That's Not My Problem!

Written by
Stephen Rickard

Illustrated by
Alan Brown

On Monday, Ella left her ruler at home.

"That's not my problem," said Dave. "You can't have my ruler – I need it."

"It's OK, Ella," said Shan. "You can borrow my ruler."

On Tuesday, Josh left his packed lunch at home.

"That's not my problem!" said Dave. "I've got **my** packed lunch."

"Don't worry, Josh," said Ella. "Shan and I will share our lunch with you. There's plenty of food for three people."

On Wednesday, Shan lost his pencil. It fell through a hole in his pocket.

"Huh! That's got nothing to do with me," said Dave.

"I've got two pencils. I can lend you one," said Josh.

On Thursday, Amir forgot his shin pads. He couldn't play football after school.

"That's not my problem!" said Dave. "I've got my shin pads, so I can play football."

"It's OK," said Shan. "I have a spare pair of pads. You can use them."

On Friday, Dave left his school bag at home.

It had his ruler, his packed lunch, his pencil and his shin pads in it.

"Oh no," said Dave. "I have no ruler or pencil for school. I have nothing to eat for lunch and I can't play football after school."

"That's not our problem!" said Ella, Shan, Josh and Amir.

"But we will help you anyway."

So Ella let Dave borrow her ruler.

Amir and Josh shared their lunch with Dave.

Shan let Dave borrow his pencil.

Amir let Dave borrow his spare shin pads.

"Thank you all," said Dave. "You have all helped me and now I don't have a problem. You are all very kind friends!" he said with a smile.

And Dave gave everybody a big hug.

His friends had looked after him, and now he'd look after them.